Poppy
the Pirate Dog

by Liz Kessler
(and Poppy)

Illustrated by
Mike Phillips

Orion
Children's Books

First published in Great Britain in 2012
by Orion Children's Books
a division of the Orion Publishing Group Ltd
Orion House
5 Upper St Martin's Lane
London WC2H 9EA
An Hachette UK Company

1 3 5 7 9 10 8 6 4 2

The Orion Publishing Group's policy is to use papers that
are natural, renewable and recyclable products and made
from wood grown in sustainable forests. The logging and
manufacturing processes are expected to conform to the
environmental regulations of the country of origin.

A catalogue record for this book
is available from the British Library

Printed in China

www.orionbooks.co.uk

*This book is dedicated to
the one and only, real life,
Poppy the Pirate Dog*

Contents

Chapter One

Something exciting was happening
at Number 12, Parkview Lane.
    The Brown family were going on
holiday.

Mum and Dad had such busy jobs that they could hardly remember how long it was since their last holiday.

Suzy and Tim Brown could remember *exactly* how long it was.

Eleven months, three weeks, two days and four hours.

And that was quite long enough.

Poppy, their two-year-old Dalmatian, agreed.

So when Dad opened the car boot
and called to her, Poppy was out of the
front door, down the path and inside
the car before you could say 'Watch
the tulips!'

Dad laughed. 'I guess we're ready
to go then,' he said.

Poppy looked out of the window as
they drove, wagging her tail all
the way.

13

'We're here!' Dad said.
Let's go and explore.'

Suzy fetched her
bucket and spade.

Tim grabbed his football
and frisbee.

Dad got his book.

Mum took her bag.

Poppy picked up
her lead.

And off they went.

'Look – a hat shop!' Mum said, as they walked along the harbour front. 'Anyone want a sun hat?'

Tim and Suzy waited outside with Poppy while Mum tried on hats and Dad said, 'Yes, that one looks lovely, dear,' lots of times.

Poppy had never been to the seaside before, but she had heard about it. And now she could see it – and smell it! She wanted a closer look. She pulled on her lead, and ran right into a nearby hat stand.

A scarf fell off the stand. It was
black, with skulls and crossbones.
Suzy picked it up.

Poppy sat at Suzy's feet and looked
at her with her big brown eyes.

'You want the scarf, do you?'
Suzy asked.

Poppy wagged her tail.

So Dad bought the skull and crossbones scarf, along with Mum's new hat. Suzy rolled up the scarf, wrapped it around Poppy's neck and tied it in a knot.

'Suits her,' Mum said.

'Very smart,' Dad agreed.

'She's a pirate!' Tim said.

'A pirate dog!' Suzy added.

'Poppy the Pirate Dog!' they all said together.

Chapter Two

Poppy knew all about pirates. Tim had five books about them, and she had spent many hours curled up on a bean bag, looking at the pictures with him.

Pirates were exciting, daring,
dangerous people. And now she was
a pirate dog!

She looked down her nose at other
dogs who came to sniff and play with
her as they walked along the harbour
front. Don't mess with me, she thought.
I'm Poppy the Pirate Dog.

When they stopped at the end
of the pier to eat ice creams, she sat
leaning against a bench and looked
out to sea. I'm looking for my pirate
ship, she thought to herself. Pirate dogs
always had their own pirate ships.

'Now what?' asked Dad, as they finished eating their ice creams. He'd had mint choc chip and he'd spilled a bit of it on his chin.

'Let's go and look at those notices on the harbour wall,' Mum said.

'Boat trips!' Suzy and Tim said, as they stood in front of the notices.

'Fishing trip – that sounds good,' Dad said.

'Seal spotting,' said Mum. 'That could be fun.'

'Pedal boats!' shouted Suzy.

'Speed boat rides!' yelled Tim.

Mum and Dad looked at each
other. 'Which one shall we do?' asked
Mum.

'Why don't we do them all?' Dad
said. 'One each day?'

Suzy and Tim threw their arms around him. Mum kissed his cheek. Poppy wagged her tail so hard she swatted a seagull.

Four boat trips! Life didn't get better than that for a pirate dog.

Chapter Three

Next morning, Poppy was first up.

She sat by the front
door, wagging her tail.

Then she ran around in circles
fifty times.

Then she nudged open Mum and
Dad's bedroom door and crept inside.
'Go away, Poppy. It's only six
o'clock!' Dad shouted.

After breakfast, everybody went down to the harbour for the boat ride. Today was the fishing trip.

They waited in the queue at the top of the harbour steps. A woman behind them stroked Poppy. 'Lovely dog,' she said.

'Nice scarf,' her husband said.

Tim smiled. 'She's a pirate dog,' he said.

When they reached the front of the queue, the fishing boat man took their tickets. 'Will she be all right on water?' he asked, looking at Poppy.

'Well, she's never done it before, but I'm sure she'll be fine,' said Mum.

'Of course she'll be fine,' Suzy said. 'She's a pirate dog!'

Dad climbed across to the fishing boat. Mum went next. Tim followed, and Suzy came last with Poppy.

'Come on, Poppy,' she said, gently tugging on Poppy's lead.

Poppy stopped at the bottom of the harbour steps.

She looked at the boat. It was bobbing up and down on the water. Sometimes it was a lot higher than her head.

Sometimes a lot lower. The sea was very rough today.

Tim took the lead from Suzy and
pulled. 'I'll do it,' he said.

Poppy took a step back.

Then she sat down.

'Let me do it,' Mum said. She took the lead from Tim and pulled harder. 'Come on, Poppy,' she said. 'There are people waiting. Jump.'

Poppy growled.

'Right. I'll sort it,' said Dad. He got off the boat, put his big arms underneath Poppy and heaved her onto the boat.

All the other holiday makers climbed aboard. The ropes were off. The engine was going. The fishing rods came out.

'We're on the open sea now, Poppy,'
Tim said.

Poppy hid in a corner of the boat,
shaking and trembling so much she
nearly fell over.

'What's the matter with her?' Suzy
asked.

'Maybe she doesn't like the sea,' Tim
said. 'It is a little bit choppy, after all.'

I'm a pirate dog, Poppy thought. Of course I like the sea!

Then a wave sprayed water over the side of the boat and the floor got all slippy, and she ran under a bench. She stayed there for the whole trip.

'Well, that was fun, wasn't it?' Dad said, as they walked back along the harbour front.

'Fish for dinner!' Mum said.

Poppy wobbled along behind them, her tail dangling between her legs. She didn't feel very well. She didn't really want to think about dinner.

Maybe fishing trips weren't the kind of thing pirate dogs enjoyed doing.

Chapter Four

That night, Poppy dreamed about adventures on the sea.

The wind in her ears, the salt on her
lips, she stood at the front of the boat,
looking ahead, and pointing a paw at
the enemy ships.

By the time she woke up in the morning, she had forgotten about yesterday. It wasn't really my kind of boat, she told herself. After all, it was a big old fishing boat. Not a pirate ship.

'Do you think we should leave her at home today?' asked Mum.

Poppy let out a whimper and jumped up to grab her lead.

'I think she wants to come,' Tim said.

They went down to the harbour,
and waited for the seal spotting trip.
This boat was newer. Poppy thought it
looked nicer.

As they made their way to the front of the queue, Poppy hoped no one would notice that her tail had stopped wagging. *I'm excited*, she told herself. Although she didn't normally shake when she was excited.

'Hey, look at that,' the seal trip
man said, pointing at Poppy's scarf.
'We've got a pirate on the trip today.'

'That's right,' Suzy said. 'She's
Poppy the Pirate Dog.'

The seal trip man smiled. 'On you get
then, Poppy the Pirate Dog,' he said.

Poppy's heart beat so fast she thought it was going to explode. But she couldn't do it again. She had to get on board. The sea was much calmer today.

She held her breath, closed her eyes...and leaped!

Poppy stood with a paw on the rail
and a pirate's scowl on her face. Don't
mess with me, she thought. I'm
a pirate dog.

This was more like it. This was
where she belonged. Out on the open
water. She was strong. She was brave.
She was…

Aaarrrggghhhhh!!
What was that??!?

'Tim, look at Poppy,' Suzy said, pointing under the bench. 'She's shaking. I think she's scared.'

Scared? Poppy thought. I'm a pirate dog! I don't get scared. Anyway, you'd be scared if you'd seen what I've just seen. An enormous sea monster that's about to swallow our boat in one gulp!

'Aww, look, Suzy,' Tim called from the side of the boat. He was pointing at the sea monster.

Don't point at it – it'll eat you! Poppy thought.

Suzy looked to where Tim was pointing.

'A cute little seal!' she said.

Poppy decided that seal-spotting trips were not the kind of thing pirate dogs enjoyed doing.

Chapter Five

'Wake up, Poppy!' Tim called. 'It's pedal boats today!'

Poppy dragged herself out of her bed and followed the Browns down to the harbour. Maybe pedal boats would be the perfect boats for pirate dogs.

'Are we really taking Poppy on a pedal boat?' Mum asked.

'We've got to. She's a pirate dog!' said Suzy and Tim.

But it turned out that going on pedal boats wasn't really the kind of thing pirate dogs liked doing.

And on Wednesday, Poppy
discovered that speed boats weren't
the kind of boats pirate dogs liked
either.

Thursday was a beach day.

Everyone on the sand was smiling and happy. But when Tim kicked a ball for her, Poppy didn't bother to chase it.

When Dad threw a frisbee, she just watched it float past her.

When Suzy stroked her, she didn't even wag her tail.

And when Mum put out her dinner
that night, she gave it two sniffs and
went back to bed.

'What's the matter with Poppy?'
Suzy and Tim asked. 'Do you think
she's ill?'

'She probably ate a dead crab on the beach and it's upset her stomach,' Dad said.

Next day, Poppy didn't even get out of bed when it was time to go to the beach.

And on Saturday, when Dad
opened the car boot for her to get in,
he had to lift her up and carry her.
Poppy slept all the way home.

Chapter Six

Back home, Poppy was miserable.
She slept all day. She walked sadly
with her head down. She hardly ever
wagged her tail.

The Browns decided to take her to the vet.

'She's as right as rain,' the vet said. He stroked her fur as he examined her. 'Nice scarf.'

'She's a pirate dog,' Suzy said glumly.

And that was when she realised!

She ran out of the vet's, pulling
Poppy along behind her. 'Mum, Dad, I
know what's the matter with her!' she
said. 'She's a pirate dog! We have to
find her the perfect pirate ship!'

At this, Poppy's ears pricked up.
Her tail flicked sideways in a tiny wag.

Tim pointed at Poppy's tail. 'I think
you might be right!' he said. 'How will
we find her the perfect pirate ship?'

'I don't know,' Suzy said. 'But we've
got to try.'

That night, the family sat round the kitchen table, looking at magazines and pictures, trying to find a pirate ship.

Suddenly, Mum jumped up.

'I've got it!' she said. 'Just the thing!'

Saturday morning came, and they all got into the car.

Poppy was nervous. What if the same thing happened again? What if she *never* found her perfect pirate ship?

Here we are,' the man from the boat company said. He pointed at their ship. 'There she is,' he said.

'She's a beauty,' Dad said.

Suzy turned to Poppy. 'What do you think?' she asked.

Poppy trotted over to the boat. She looked back at her family and lifted her ears. This looked more like her kind of pirate ship!

Tim nodded. 'Go on, get on board,' he said.

Poppy stepped across the large wooden plank on to the boat.

She stood on the back deck, wagging her tail. She bounced inside and ran up and down the boat.

She poked her head through the front doors and jumped onto the front deck.

'Look!' Suzy called, pointing at Poppy's tail.

It was wagging so hard it nearly knocked a plant pot off the deck.

Dad started the engine.

Poppy proudly took her place on her pirate ship.

Suzy sat next to Poppy and stroked her ears as the boat began its journey.

'We've found your perfect pirate ship,' Suzy whispered.

You certainly have, Poppy thought. It's exactly the right size, it's not too fast, and there are no sea monsters.

The pirate ship swished through the water at its top speed.

This is exactly the kind of ship a pirate dog likes, Poppy thought.

And then she curled up in a tight ball, shuffled a bit closer to the wood-burning stove, stretched, yawned, and went to sleep.